Ollie's Birthday Surprise

Nicola Killen

SIMON & SCHUSTER
London   New York   Sydney   Toronto   New Delhi

It was Ollie's birthday and she had been
very excited to open her presents.
A new tiger suit was just what
she'd wished for!

As she ran round the house
practising her roar,

Ollie suddenly froze. The biggest bunch of balloons
she'd ever seen was floating by!

Dashing outside as fast as she could, Ollie gave chase.

Each time she got close,

Whoosh!

A gust of wind pushed the
balloons beyond her grasp.

Ready to give up and go home,
she stood still for a moment.

But then she remembered . . .

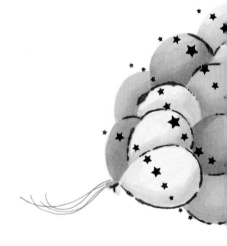

... she was a tiger!

She raced on, through the meadow

Roar!

Down the dusty track

Rooaar!!

And along the river bank

Roooaaarrr!!!

With the balloons almost in reach,
Ollie gave the biggest

ROOAARR!!!

she could and leapt forward.

She gasped as the ground quickly moved away
from beneath her feet.

She was flying!

Houses, trees and fields passed below,
before the wind dropped and she floated down...

As she landed, Ollie's attention was
drawn to a gap between the trees.

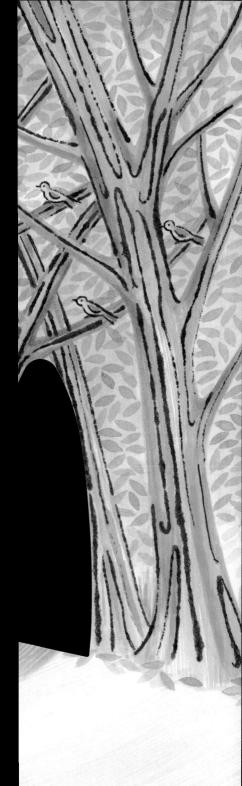

ff down the path,
d her.

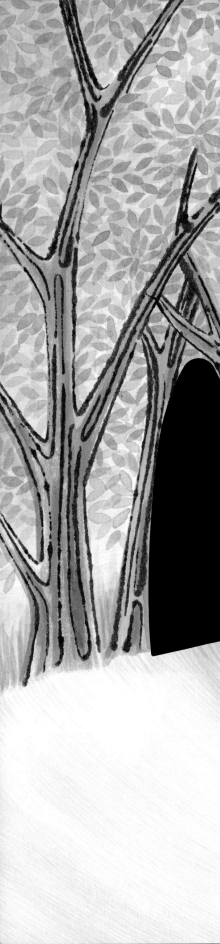

What was going on in there?

Determined to find out, she sped off do
balloons trailing behind he

BIRTHDAY, OLLIE!

Ollie stopped, stunned by what she'd found –
a surprise party just for her!

Once everyone had wished Ollie a happy
birthday, it was time to play some games.

Bear gave out clues for a treasure hunt and the search began.

There was so much to find!

Then it was pass-the-parcel.
The birds sang the stop-start music beautifully.

There were lots and lots of layers to unwrap
and some fantastically funny prizes!

Musical statues was just as enjoyable.

Monkey couldn't keep still

and Ollie laughed so hard that she was out, too!!

Sloth was the winner – he didn't move at all.

Next, each animal took a turn blowing bubbles,
while everyone else tried to burst them.

Pop!

Pop!

Pop!

It was the best fun ever!

When all the games had been played,
Elephant helped them cool off.

Now they were ready for a delicious birthday lunch. Yummy!

As Ollie blew out her candles, all the animals sang Happy Birthday *really* loudly!
She closed her eyes and wished she could be a tiger every day!

Before she said goodbye, Ollie thanked everyone for her wonderful party.

Drifting gently home,
she felt incredibly lucky

and as her feet
touched the ground
she gave a joyful

Roar!

This had been a birthday
she would always remember!